Tundra Books, an imprint of Penguin Random House Canada Young Readers,
a Penguin Random House Company

Library and Archives Canada Cataloguing in Publication

Flouw, Benjamin
[Milléclat dorée. English]
      The golden glow / Benjamin Flouw.

Translation of: La milléclat dorée.
Issued in print and electronic formats.
ISBN 978-0-7352-6412-0 (hardcover).—ISBN 978-0-7352-6413-7 (EPUB)

      I. Title. II. Title: Milléclat dorée. English.

PZ23.F56Gol 2018   j843'.92   C2017-904324-2
                                                C2017-904325-0

Published simultaneously in the United States of America by Tundra Books of Northern New York,
an imprint of Penguin Random House Canada Young Readers, a Penguin Random House Company

Originally published in 2017 by La Pastèque

Library of Congress Control Number: 2017945602

Acquired by Tara Walker
English edition edited by Peter Phillips
English translation by Christelle Morelli and Susan Ouriou
The artwork in this book is a mixture of digital painting and hand-painted textures.
The text is set in Linotte.
Texture on title type © Nik Merkulov/Shutterstock.com

Printed and bound in China

www.penguinrandomhouse.ca

1 2 3 4 5   22 21 20 19 18

Penguin
Random House
tundra | TUNDRA BOOKS

THE GOLDEN GLOW

Benjamin Flouw

Translated by Christelle Morelli and Susan Ouriou

tundra

Every evening, sitting in his armchair, Fox likes to leaf through old botany books, looking for the next new plant to add to his collection.

What's this? A page with no picture!

The golden glow is a plant from the Wellhidden family.
It is very rare and only grows high in the mountains.
No specimen has ever been described.

"This sounds like a fabulously fascinating flower!
Tomorrow, I'm off to the mountain in search of it!"

BOTANY

Before bedtime, Fox gets his backpack ready, making sure not to forget:

a map

a snack
(grape pâté sandwiches, his favorite)

a notebook

a pencil

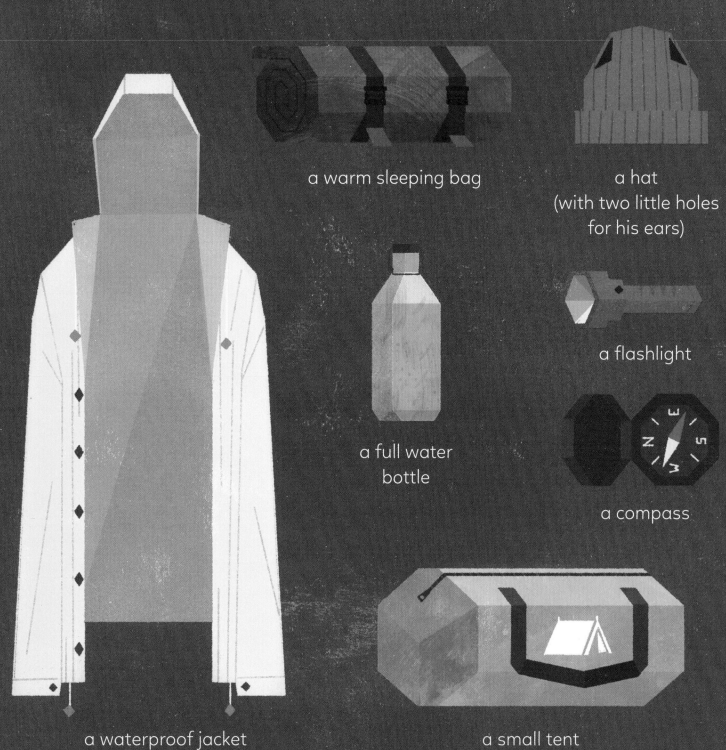

a warm sleeping bag

a hat
(with two little holes
for his ears)

a full water
bottle

a flashlight

a compass

a waterproof jacket

a small tent

The sun isn't even up yet, but Fox is ready!
He has a long day's walk ahead of him.

With his trusty compass and map in hand,
there's no danger that he'll get lost

The forest is quiet and peaceful first thing in the morning.
Only a few birds are awake and chirping.

Fox studies the plants and trees that line the path.
They're all ones he's seen before.

He knows the name of each tree he
walks under:

Here's a fir tree.

There's an oak.

This one's a beech tree

. . . and that one's a spruce.

Next is the ash tree,

then the famous maple

. . . and last is the sturdy larch.

As he nears a riverbank,
Fox catches sight of Bear,
leisurely fishing for salmon.

"Good morning, Bear! Maybe you can help me. I'm on the hunt for the golden glow, a fabulously fascinating flower. I don't know what it looks like, but I do know it's very rare."

"Every day, I come to the river to fish and every day I see the same flowers. Most of them are beautiful, but none of them are rare. You should talk to Marmot. She knows all of the mountain's plants. But she isn't easy to find."

Fox looks under slabs of rock,

inside hollow stumps,

and in old earthen burrows,

but . . . no Marmot.

Where can she be hiding?

It's almost noon and Fox is hungry. He sits on a fallen log and pulls one of his grape pâté sandwiches out of his backpack.

A snout pokes out from the bush across the way, followed by two pointy ears. Its nostrils sniff the air for a whiff of the irresistible grape pâté.

Fox recognizes his cousin Wolf right away and invites him over to share his snack.

"I've never seen the golden glow, Fox. But I do know where to find Marmot. As soon as I'm done with this delicious sandwich, I'll take you to her. I'm as hungry as a wolf!"

After a long trek through the forest, Fox and Wolf finally reach a large steep clearing dotted with flowers of every color.

No need for an encyclopedia here!
Fox can name all of them:

anemones

purple saxifrage

violets

veronica

moss campion

mountain sorrel

mountain avens

forget-me-not

butterwort

Placing a long blade of grass split
down the middle onto his lips,
Wolf sounds a shrill whistle . . .

and Marmot pops out from behind a rock!

"The golden glow! Yes, I have seen it! Beautiful! Unforgettable! But rare! You have to climb right to the top! To the summit!"

Fox sets off again, leaving Wolf
and Marmot behind. He walks
quickly, excited to be so close
to his goal at last.

Little by little, billowing clouds fill the sky.
Fox climbs so high that he finds himself
stumbling through a dense fog.

Suddenly, a strange shape looms into view . . .

It's Mountain Goat, balanced on a boulder, reading a book.

"There's no point going any higher, Fox.
Nothing grows at that altitude! But if you're
bound and determined, take this walking
stick to help."

Fox has already climbed a good portion of the mountain,
but the hardest part is yet to come.

snow zone

9800 ft

alpine zone

8200 ft

subalpine zone

6200 ft

montane zone

3300 ft

foothill zone

Even so, Fox doesn't get discouraged, and soon he's made his way out of the clouds to be greeted by the sun.

But he finds not a single flower on the summit. Nothing but rocks and snow.

The day is fast drawing to a close.
Fox has to hurry to set up camp before nightfall.

Once he's pitched his tent and rolled out his sleeping bag,
Fox sits himself down to watch the sun set.

As he lays his walking stick on the ground,
he feels something brush against his paw . . .

Hidden under the snow is a fabulously fascinating flower.
It must be the golden glow!

Just as he reaches over to pick the flower, Fox changes his mind.

This golden glow is more beautiful here on the mountaintop than it ever would be in a vase in his living room.

He opens his backpack and pulls out his notebook and pencil.

Then, studying the plant from every angle, he begins to draw.

His pencil takes note of every detail:

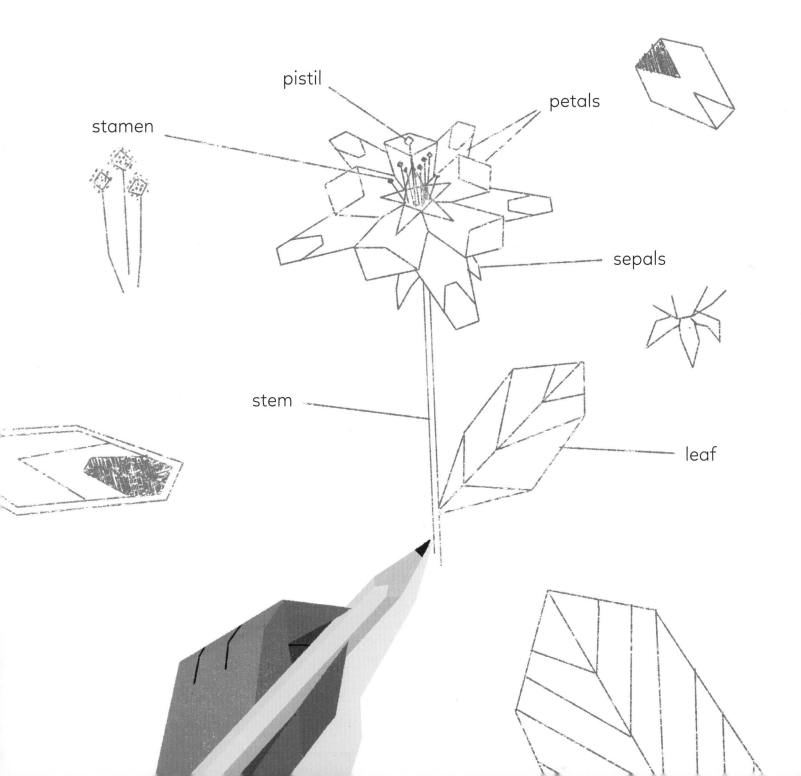

stamen

pistil

petals

sepals

stem

leaf

Back home the next day, he'll put all of his
drawings into his botany book so that . . .

. . . in the evening, sitting in his armchair, he will never forget just how fabulously fascinating his golden glow is, high up on the mountaintop.